Dear Parents,

Welcome to the Scholastic Reader series. We have taken over 80 years of experience with teachers, parents, and children and put it into a program that is designed to match your child's interests and skills.

Level 1—Short sentences and stories made up of words kids can sound out using their phonics skills and words that are important to remember.

Level 2—Longer sentences and stories with words kids need to know and new "big" words that they will want to know.

Level 3—From sentences to paragraphs to longer stories, these books have large "chunks" of texts and are made up of a rich vocabulary.

Level 4—First chapter books with more words and fewer pictures.

It is important that children learn to read well enough to succeed in school and beyond. Here are ideas for reading this book with your child:

- Look at the book together. Encourage your child to read the title and make a prediction about the story.
- Read the book together. Encourage your child to sound out words when appropriate. When your child struggles, you can help by providing the word.
- Encourage your child to retell the story. This is a great way to check for comprehension.
- Have your child take the fluency test on the last page to check progress.

Scholastic Readers are designed to support your child's efforts to learn how to read at every age and every stage. Enjoy helping your child learn to read and love to read.

—**Francie Alexander**
Chief Education Officer
Scholastic Education

Copyright © 1999 by Norman Bridwell.
Activities copyright © 2003 Scholastic Inc.
All rights reserved. Published by Scholastic Inc.
SCHOLASTIC, CARTWHEEL BOOKS, and associated logos
are trademarks and/or registered trademarks of Scholastic Inc.
CLIFFORD, CLIFFORD THE BIG RED DOG, and associated logos are
trademarks and/or registered trademarks of Norman Bridwell.

Library of Congress Cataloging-in-Publication Data is available.

ISBN: 0-439-09834-3

10 9 8 7 6 5   06 07 08
Printed in the U.S.A. 23 • First printing, October 1999

Norman Bridwell
CLIFFORD®
AND THE
HALLOWEEN
PARADE

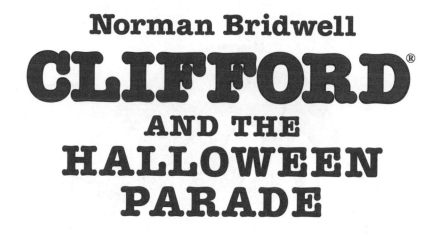

Scholastic Reader — Level 1

SCHOLASTIC INC.

New York   Toronto   London   Auckland   Sydney
Mexico City   New Delhi   Hong Kong   Buenos Aires

Clifford sees a bat.

Clifford sees a cat.

Clifford sees a rat.

It is Halloween!
What will Clifford be?

A boy brings a ladder.

A girl brings a hose.

The boy brings a light that flashes.

Here comes the boy in a
raincoat, hat, and boots.

Here comes the girl in a raincoat, hat, and boots.

They climb on Clifford.

Clifford is a fire engine.
The boy and girl are firefighters.

The Halloween parade will soon begin.

The boy, the girl, and Clifford come first.
Then come the bat, the cat, and the rat.

Happy Halloween, everybody!

• Word List •

a	hat
and	here
are	hose
bat	in
be	is
begin	it
boots	ladder
boy	light
brings	on
cat	parade
Clifford	raincoat
climb	rat
comes	sees
engine	soon
everybody	that
fire	the
firefighters	then
first	they
flashes	today
girl	what
Halloween	will
happy	